MAYANS: 1
TIME WARP TRIO: 0

"We do know a few tricks," I said to the High Priest. "But we're not really magicians. We're three guys who got sent here by a magic *Book* we don't really know how to work. We just have to find it. Then we'll take off right out of here, and you guys can get back to your sacred ball game. So have you seen anything that looks like a thin blue *Book*?"

The High Priest looked at us. He looked around at the crowd of people in the ring ball court. He seemed to be thinking what to do. Then he yelled, "Seize them! We will sacrifice them to the harvest!"

Warriors with spears and knives surrounded us.

"That went well," said Sam. His eyes rolled up, and he fell to the ground.

ME OH MAYA

THE TIME WARP TRIO®

THE TIME WARP TRIO

No. 13

ME OH MAYA

JON SCIESZKA

illustrated by Adam McCauley

PUFFIN BOOKS

PUFFIN BOOKS

Published by the Penguin Group

Penguin Young Readers Group, 345 Hudson Street, New York, New York 10014, U.S.A.

Penguin Group (Canada), 90 Eglinton Avenue East, Suite 700, Toronto, Ontario, Canada
M4P 2Y3 (a division of Pearson Penguin Canada Inc.)

Penguin Books Ltd, 80 Strand, London WC2R 0RL, England

Penguin Ireland, 25 St Stephen's Green, Dublin 2, Ireland (a division of Penguin Books Ltd)

Penguin Group (Australia), 250 Camberwell Road, Camberwell,
Victoria 3124, Australia (a division of Pearson Australia Group Pty Ltd)

Penguin Books India Pvt Ltd, 11 Community Centre,
Panchsheel Park, New Delhi - 110 017, India

Penguin Group (NZ), Cnr Airborne and Rosedale Roads, Albany, Auckland 1310,
New Zealand (a division of Pearson New Zealand Ltd)

Penguin Books (South Africa) (Pty) Ltd, 24 Sturdee Avenue, Rosebank,
Johannesburg 2196, South Africa

Registered Offices: Penguin Books Ltd, 80 Strand, London WC2R 0RL, England

First published in the United States of America by Viking,
a division of Penguin Young Readers Group, 2003
Published by Puffin Books, a division of Penguin Young Readers Group, 2006

9 10

Text copyright © Jon Scieszka, 2003
Illustrations copyright © Penguin Group (USA) Inc., 2003
Illustrations by Adam McCauley

THE LIBRARY OF CONGRESS HAS CATALOGED THE VIKING EDITION AS FOLLOWS:
Scieszka, Jon.
Me oh Maya / by Jon Sciezka ; illustrated by Adam McCauley.
p. cm.
Summary: Joe, Fred, and Sam find themselves whisked by The Book to the
main ring-ball court in Chichen Itza, Mexico in 1000 A.D., where they
must play for their lives against a Mayan High Priest who cheats.
ISBN 0-670-03629-3
[1. Time travel—Fiction. 2. Magic—Fiction. 3. Ball games—Fiction. 4. Mayas—Fiction.
5. Indians of Mexico—Fiction. 6. Mexico—History—To 1810—Fiction.
7. Humorous stories.] I. McCauley, Adam, ill. II. Title.
PZ7.S41267Me 2003 [Fic]—dc21 2003010319

Puffin Books ISBN 0-14-240300-8

The Time Warp Trio ® is a registered trademark of Penguin Group (USA) Inc.

Printed in the United States of America
Set in Sabon

To Dan Feigin and Peter Feigin—
the two most do-or-die ringball
players I know.
J. S.

For Wigmamma, El Tigre,
and Merida.
A. M.

•

(one)

"How dare you interrupt the sacred game!"

"Huh?" said Fred. He tucked his basketball under one arm.

I knew we weren't in Brooklyn anymore. But that's about all I knew. It was hot. The sky was bright blue.

Fred, Sam, and I were standing in the middle of some kind of courtyard surrounded by tall stone walls. A short brown-skinned guy in a wild feathered headdress stood on top of the wall looking down at us. The four players of the game we had interrupted stood eyeing us. They wore padded belts, leg and shoulder pads, and not much else.

"Explain yourselves or your blood will be spilled in sacrifice," said the feathered guy.

"Where the heck are we now?" said Fred. "I was just about to win it all."

1

"No way," said Sam.

"Totally," said Fred.

"Not likely," said Sam.

"*Silence*, invaders!" yelled Feather Guy. "I am the High Priest of Chichén Itzá. I will rip your hearts out. Answer."

"Did he say 'Chicken Pizza'?" said Fred.

"Chichén Itzá," said Sam. He looked around at the crowd of people watching the game from each

end of the courtyard. "It's the name of the city built by those people I was telling you about . . . before we got warped here by someone who wasn't being careful with *The Book*." Sam gave me a look. "We're in a Maya ring ball court, about a thousand years ago."

"So that's good news, right?" I said.

Sam adjusted his glasses. "Except for their habit of sacrificing humans." Sam squinted up at the High Priest. "He's not kidding about that rip-your-hearts-out."

"Whoa," I said. "That is definitely not good." I turned to the High Priest. "Mr. High Priest, I am Joe. This is Sam. He's Fred. We come from uh . . . a place called Brooklyn. We are very powerful magicians."

The High Priest stepped back. "Makers of magic?" He sounded afraid.

"Oh yeah," I said. "You don't want to mess with sacrificing us."

Sam groaned. "Not again. This never works. Have you ever noticed that when we time warp, we usually get into more trouble with our tricks?"

"Have you got a better idea?" I asked.

"Yeah. Let's tell them who we really are. Tell

them we just need to get *The Book*, and then get out of here," said Sam.

"Like that will work," said Fred. "I say we fight our way out of here. You guys take the two in the blue feathers. I'll take care of the red-feather team."

"What magic do you know?" asked the High Priest.

I thought about trying one of my new coin tricks. Maybe a rope trick. Then I thought about what Sam had said. I was kind of insulted. But you know what? Sam did have a point. Our tricks did seem to get us into more trouble. I decided to give Sam's idea a try. I decided to try to get through an entire time warp without using a single trick.

"We do know a few tricks," I said to the High Priest. "But we're not really magicians. We're three guys who got sent here by a magic *Book* we don't really know how to work. We just have to find it. Then we'll take off right out of here, and you guys can get back to your sacred ball game. So have you seen anything that looks like a thin blue *Book*?"

The High Priest looked at us. He looked around at the crowd of people in the ring ball court. He seemed to be thinking what to do. Then he yelled, "Seize them! We will sacrifice them to the harvest!"

Warriors with spears and knives surrounded us.

"That went well," said Sam. His eyes rolled up, and he fell to the ground.

••
(two)

But before we donate blood—all of our blood—to the Maya harvest, I would like to try to explain how three guys from Brooklyn could get into such a mess one thousand years ago in Mexico.

It all started with a game of H-O-R-S-E. You know—the basketball game. The one where you take turns shooting. The guy after you has to make the shot you make, or get a letter. Get all the letters, you are a horse, and you are out.

You can play the game to spell out any word. But we got in trouble last week with the new teacher in the school yard for even saying those words. So I'm not going to write them down. But that's a whole other story. Back to this story.

I can almost hear you thinking, "I've played H-O-R-S-E before. It never got me sacrificed."

But you don't have a certain book. A thin blue book covered with twisting silver symbols and de-

6

signs. A book given to you by your uncle Joe the magician (who's not really a very good magician). A book that can somehow, someway warp you to any time or place.

That's the difference. I have that book. It's called *The Book*. And so far it's managed to warp Sam and Fred and me all over time and space.

We've seen everything from Stone Age cave people to our own great-granddaughters one hundred years in the future. We've wrestled gladiators. We've sailed with pirates. We've hung out with the guy who built the Brooklyn Bridge.

We've just never figured out exactly how *The Book* works. A picture, a word, a drawing, even a haiku poem can trigger *The Book*'s green time warping mist. We do know that the only way to get back to our time is to find *The Book* in the time we travel to. We have no idea how to keep track of *The Book*.

One of these days we might have to actually read *The Book* and see if it has any directions.

But this day was so nice and sunny. We'd been stuck in school all day. We had to get outside and play some basketball. Sam and Fred and I met up at the hoops near Fred's house.

"Dead, you guys are both D-E-A-D after this next incredible shot," said Fred. He twisted his new Knicks hat backward on his head. He stood behind the three-point line.

"Airball," said Sam, not even looking up. He was doodling on the blacktop with a piece of chalk. Sam and I both had H-O-R-S. Fred had H.

"Did you just call me a hairball?" said Fred.

Sam drew a group of dots and lines. "Did you know that the ancient Maya people who lived one thousand years ago had this number system every bit as good as ours, and a calendar that was even better?"

Fred and I hardly noticed what he said at the time. Sam always comes up with stuff like this.

One week he's an expert on World War Two submarines. The next week it's samurai warriors. You can always learn something new listening to Sam . . . even if it's just a really bad joke.

"No," said Fred. "But I know you two are about to become ancient history with this shot." Fred hefted the ball in one hand. "One bounce, off the backboard, cash money kick butt in your face."

"Knucklehead says what?" said Sam.

Fred held his shooting pose. "You're not going to trick me into saying 'what.'"

"You just said it."

"What?"

"Knucklehead."

"Come on you guys," I said. "I'm going to need a calendar to time your shots if they're any slower. Shoot the ball, you big zero."

"And speaking of zeroes," said Sam, "the Maya also invented zero. They wrote it like this."

Sam drew on the blacktop:

"That's fascinating, Professor Loser," said Fred, lining up his shot.

"They used a dot for one, a line for five, and

counted in groups of twenty. So this was eight:

Fred dribbled the ball once, twice.
"This was twenty-eight":

Fred aimed the ball.
"So today's date, 9/22/2003, would be written in Maya numerals":

Sam drew the last dot.
Fred bounced the ball for his shot.
We heard a small pop in my

backpack under the hoop. A familiar curl of green mist snuck out from under the flap on my pack.

Fred's shot rose up, and up, and—

The green mist snake suddenly grew and swallowed us. We spun twisting, dropping, and time warping through thousands of pages of calendar time. And we were gone from 9/22/2003.

• • •
(three)

Guys with bright colored feather headpieces and long white loincloths grabbed our arms. Other guys poked sharp green stone blade spears in our chests. Someone swiped Fred's ball from him. They stood Sam up and slapped him awake.

It looked like they were going to do the blood sacrificing right here.

It suddenly became very hot and very still. Parrots screeched in the jungle behind the stone wall. Monkeys screamed. Bugs buzzed. You know how they say you can hear your heart pounding? Now I know what they mean.

The High Priest came down to stand in front of us. He did not look like a happy guy. But he definitely dressed nice. He had on the fanciest outfit of anyone, I guess to show he was the boss. His feathered head thing was the biggest and brightest. He wore a huge green stone skull necklace. Hoops

hung from his ears. A cape of spotted animal skin hung over one shoulder. Tattoos covered both legs.

He was short with dark brown skin, black hair, and black eyes. He kind of looked like our science teacher, Mr. Ramirez, on a really, really crabby day. He looked us over, then spoke.

"Today is a very important day in our calendar. This is the battle of the day against the night. It is the day before the sign for the harvest. What can this sign of you three in the middle of our sacred ball game mean? Why these strange clothes?"

Fred, Sam, and I looked at each other. We had on our usual jeans, T-shirts, and sneakers. We looked at the High Priest. He was the one with the feathers on his head and the animal skin over his belly.

"Sorry to interrupt your game, Mr. High Priest," I said. "We wear these clothes because . . . because they help us travel fast once we find our *Book*."

The other robed and feathered priests behind the High Priest whispered to each other.

"Oh?" said the High Priest. "A book you say? So you also know reading and writing? You know numbers, and the calendar of the sun and moon and Venus?"

Sam perked up. "Oh sure. We love your number system. And your calendars—fantastic. You really are a terrific bunch of people. It's even terrific that you play your ball game with no hands. And I'm not just saying that so you don't splash our blood all over your temple or whatever. I really, really mean it. Inventing the zero and all of that, too. Amazing. Hey—maybe I could help you out with fractions?"

The High Priest nodded. "So you are definitely priests of your people. Who else would know these arts?" The other priests nodded. "You will make a most excellent sacrifice."

Sam started to wobble again.

"No, no, no," I said. "We're not priests. Sam was just kidding. He's a little crazy you know. Just look at him."

Sam's head flopped around.

"We don't really read and write that much. We're more like magic guys who bring very good luck to people . . . uh . . . only if we're alive."

The crowd around the ring ball court got restless. They started clapping and cheering. The ring ball players got restless, too. They started bouncing the ball off their hips and chests like

Sam said—with no hands. One of the players tried it with Fred's basketball. It gave me an idea. An idea where I didn't have to come up with a trick.

"We are also very famous ball players in our land," I said.

Fred and Sam gave me a funny look.

"We are here on this very important day in the calendar to show you a new shot in the battle of the day against the night."

Now the priests looked really freaked out. I figured we had nothing to lose (except maybe all of the blood pumping through our bodies). So I grabbed the basketball and passed it to Fred.

"This is Fred Kashmuny and Sam Inurface. I am Joe Kikbut. Fred will now show you his famous bounce-bank-rim shot. But in our land, we use our hands."

Fred looked at the stone ring set in the wall. It was set sideways, not level like a basketball hoop. And it looked about three times as high as a basketball hoop. Fred eyed the ring. He dribbled behind his back and through his legs while he was thinking. The Maya crowd had never seen anything like this before. They cheered and whistled.

16

The High Priest looked around at the crowd. He looked at the small stone ring. He looked at Fred.

"Yes, we will let the gods of this day decide your fate. Show us your way," said the High Priest. He smiled one of those fake smiles.

The other priests whispered back and forth some more. I could see they were not happy to have their universe messed with. Fred had to make this shot or we would lose more than a letter.

Fred twisted his Knicks cap around and bounced a few tosses off the wall to get a

"Show them how, Kashmuny," said Sam.

"One bounce, off the wall, and in," said Fred.

The High Priest raised his hands for quiet.

Fred bounced a hard two-handed overhead pass off the ground. It sailed toward the wall. It rose up and up and—

d
feel

••••
(four)

And time really can do weird things.

You think it always moves along the same. But then an hour sitting indoors on your grandma's couch stretches into days. The two weeks at the end of summer vacation shrink down to about two seconds.

There is Fred's true do-or-die shot. It's stopped in midair between chapters. No time left on the clock.

Sam's mouth hangs wide open as he watches it.

The High Priest stands with his arms folded across his chest. He's still kind of half fake-smiling, thinking no way this is ever going in.

Fred stares at the shot with the most intense look I've ever seen on his face.

And there is the ball. Perfectly round, spinning forward a little from the bounce. It hangs between red-brown ground and bright blue sky.

19

Between night and day. Between life or blood sacrifice.

The ball sails up and up and up. It kisses off the stone wall, bounces out . . . and through the stone ring without touching anything.

Ring ball swish.

The crowd screams. Parrots explode into the sky out over the jungle. The ball players bug their eyes out. Sam and I actually jump for pure joy.

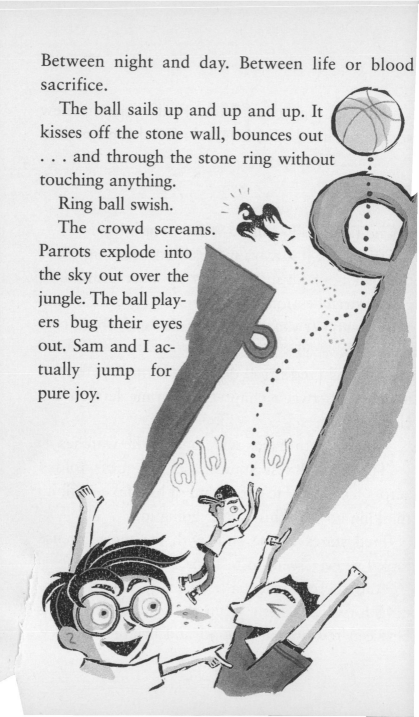

We yell, "Kashmuny, Inurface, Kikbut. Wooooo-oo!"

The ball players surround Fred to try this new style using hands. Fred shows a few dribble moves.

"Next thing you guys got to do is get that rim fixed. Turn it up the right way. Then we can work on shooting the J, see?"

Fred demonstrates his jump shot.

The Maya ball players give it a try.

The crowd cheers and cheers and cheers.

I turn to the High Priest. He still has his arms folded across his chest. He still has that fake smile stuck on his face. Though now his eyes are flashing like lightning.

"Very interesting," he says in a way that doesn't seem very interested. "Follow me."

(five)

We followed the High Priest out of the stone-walled ball court. The other priests followed us. The rest of the crowd joined in behind them. We were a regular victory parade down Broadway.

"Look at these carvings on the wall," said Sam. "A headless guy with snakes coming out of his neck."

"That's blood," said a priest with a ponytail. "He was captain of the losing team."

"Now that's what I call 'sudden death overtime,'" said Fred.

We walked out of the ring ball court into a city in the middle of a jungle. A giant stone pyramid with steps on every side rose in front of us. A smaller red stone temple stood next to it. A long covered walkway of a hundred giant stone columns led to another building. And every wall, column, and building seemed to be covered with carvings of snakes, birds, cats, and people colored red, yellow, green, and blue.

The town square in the center of the buildings was filled with people buying and selling stuff: clay pots and dishes, food, cloth, animal skins. . . . It looked like a farmer's market and a state fair all rolled into one.

The High Priest led our parade right through the middle of everything. I noticed people looked away from him, but they stared at us. We must have looked like aliens from another planet to them. I know they looked like aliens to us.

A bunch of guys about our age ran along beside us. A kid in a spotted animal skin waved. "Nice shot!" We waved back. We were celebrities. For once this looked like a time warp where we were going to be the heroes . . . instead of the punching bags.

"I smell food," said Fred.

We paraded past an old woman cooking tortillas and roasting three small birds over a fire.

"Three chicken burritos to go, please," said Fred.

The High Priest led us right up the giant pyramid steps. We had to half run to keep up with him. Giant stone snake heads guarded either side of the

bottom of the steps. The crowd stayed next to the snake heads. We climbed the steps with the priests, and finally collapsed in the doorway of a little stone room at the very top.

I felt like I was going to throw up and pass out and burn up all at the same time.

"Man," said Fred. "Nothing like climbing a thousand steps to get our reward."

"Ninety-one," said Sam, still puffing. "It's a calendar thing. Four sides of ninety-one steps. Ninety-one plus ninety-one plus ninety-one plus ninety-one equals three hundred sixty-four. This last step on top equals three hundred sixty-five for the number of days in the year."

We looked out over the whole city and miles and miles of green jungle.

"So we're standing on top of a giant Maya calendar," I said.

"Freaky," said Fred.

The High Priest stood at the top of the steps. He looked down at the people at the bottom and raised his hands.

"It's about to get freakier," said Sam. "Watch this. They figured out some way to build this pyramid so every word the High Priest says from up here travels down the steps. He doesn't even have to shout."

The High Priest spoke.

"Three strangers come to us like an unexplained star in the sky." The people down below nodded. Sam was right. They could hear every word. "It is our duty as your priests to read the stars and keep the universe in balance."

The High Priest held out one hand. Another priest in fancy earrings and a necklace put a stack of thin boards covered with drawings and numbers in his hand.

"Our prize," I said. "It must be the Maya version of *The Book*."

"I can't believe it," said Sam.

The High Priest opened the book and showed it to Fred and Sam and me. We braced ourselves for a quick time travel exit.

Nothing happened.

No green time traveling mist leaked out.

I started to worry just a little bit. I figured we probably had to hold the Maya book to get it to time warp.

"Check it out, Sam," said Fred. "Dot and line numbers just like you wrote."

The High Priest held up the connected boards
that folded into a book.

"The book says that three strange ball players
will come." The High Priest turned a page. "They
will show us strange ways." He turned another
page. "They will be the perfect sacrifice for the best
harvest ever!"

28

The crowd gave a giant "Oooooh."

"Hey, wait a minute," I said. "How do you know it says that?"

"Yeah," said Fred. "It looks like it says 'Snake, bird, bird, monkey guy, bird' to me."

"You're just making that up," said Sam. "Give us *The Book*!"

"Fred made the shot," I said. "We had a deal."

Fred made a move to grab *The Book*. Three priests with wrestlers' grips pulled our arms behind our backs.

"Silence!" boomed the High Priest. "No one questions me. I am the one true High Priest—Kakapupahed!"

Now I knew we were in a life-and-death situation. And I knew we shouldn't laugh. Sam knew we shouldn't laugh. Fred knew we shouldn't laugh.

We all laughed.

"Did you just say your name was 'Caca Poopoo Head'?" said Fred.

"Kakapupahed," said all of the priests, bowing lower and lower as the High Priest got madder and madder.

We knew we shouldn't but . . . we laughed again.

(six)

Fifteen minutes later, Fred, Sam, and I weren't laughing. We were tied to a tree in the jungle. The tree stood next to a blue-green pool of water. There seemed to be a lot of white sticks on the ground. I had a bad feeling that the white sticks were actually bones.

Kakapupahed leaned his large face up close. Now he looked happy. "The sun goes down. Day becomes night. Night is the jaguar. Tomorrow, if you are still here, we will throw you in the sacred well."

"We have got to stop laughing at other people's names," said Sam.

Kakapupahed looked up into the trees. Something was moving up there. "Or maybe you will give yourselves to the snake." Kakapupahed and his priests walked over to the pool of water.

"Did he just say 'snake'?" said Fred. "Tell me he didn't say 'snake.' I really do not like snakes."

Fred looked up, panicked. Every drooping branch suddenly looked like a snake.

"We will come back for you at the first return of the sun tomorrow," said Kakapupahed. Then they were gone.

The bird, bug, and monkey chorus started up in the jungle again. We tugged against the vine ropes holding us tight to the tree. But we weren't going anywhere. The sunlight slowly dimmed in the thick jungle vines and leaves. Something dropped from a tree behind us with a meaty *thump*.

Fred twitched. "Sam, you don't think there are really snakes out here big enough to eat us, do you?"

"The—the giant anaconda is usually about fifteen feet long, but larger specimens, up to—to—to twenty-five feet have been reported," said Sam. "And I believe the anaconda is native to this area."

The something behind us rustled the dead leaves on the ground.

The sunlight faded. I strained my eyes to look in the bushes. I saw something moving toward us.

"Sam, what has yellow fur with kind of black circles with spots?" I asked.

"I know that old joke," said Sam. "And it's not that funny. And this being tied up to a tree is not that funny anymore either. Now would be a good time for one of your magic tricks, Joe. Like do something with this rope."

The same yellow-spotted something moved behind a tree. A tail stuck out.

"I'm not joking," I said.

"Well, giant anacondas are usually green with black oval dots," said Sam. "Yellow fur with circles and spots sounds more like a jaguar."

"That sounds about right," I said. The jaguar crouched behind the nearest bush. It coiled to spring

32

and make a bloody end of the Time Warp Trio.

"Sam," I said. "I always did think some of your jokes were funny. And Fred—that was a great shot."

I thought, this is the end. But at least Fred won't have to worry about snakes.

(seven)

The jaguar crept closer. He jumped into the clearing in front of us and said, "Great shot."

I think Sam passed out for just a second again. His head fell on my shoulder.

It wasn't a jaguar. It was the kid we had seen in town wearing the jaguar skin.

"What the heck?" said Fred.

The jaguar boy quickly cut through the vine ropes with his knife.

"My name is Jun. We have to hurry. My uncle will kill me if he catches me doing this."

The vines fell to the ground. Sam fell down and then jumped to his feet. "Wha'? Who? Ha?"

"Who is your uncle?" I said.

"Kakapupahed," said Jun. "And if he doesn't kill us, the jaguars really will. Come on. Run."

We didn't laugh this time. We ran. We ran down a small path twisting under jungle trees and bushes.

34

We ran following Jun's jaguar cape as the jungle got darker and spookier. We ran until we found ourselves standing inside a small mud brick house. One lamp burned in the corner. A woman with long black hair tied back with a ribbon sat on a straw mat. Jun gave her a hug.

"Mama," said Jun. "It was just like you said. They were tied to the Jaguar Tree by the pool. Why would Uncle do that? They are good ball players. They made the shot."

Jun's mom put her hand on his head. "Your uncle is a mad man. Not very smart. But very mad, and very mean. He will do anything to have power. This is why the people are afraid of him."

Jun's mom turned to us and smiled. She looked like somebody I knew. I'm not sure why, but I instantly felt safe.

"But our guests are here. Welcome, boys. Sit down. You must be hungry."

"Starving," said Fred.

Jun's mom laid out a spread of tortillas with corn and beans and tomatoes and peppers. I had been too freaked out to notice, but Fred was right, we were starving. We ate until we were full. Then Jun's mom brought out clay cups. We took a sip. It was chocolate and vanilla and honey.

"A special drink for our honored guests," said Jun's mom.

We drank. And then she told us the most terrible story.

Jun's mom and dad had been nobles in the city of Chichén Itzá. Her family had been high officials in the city for years. Jun's dad was a famous ball player for the city.

Kakapupahed was Jun's mom's younger brother. He was always a brat, and had to be in charge. He was jealous of Jun's mom and Jun's dad. He was also a pretty bad ball player, but thought he was great.

I forget how Jun's mom said it exactly. She was very quiet. And you could tell it still made her sad. But she said Kakapupahed fixed a ball game so Jun's dad would lose, and old Kakapupahed would become the single High Priest.

Jun's dad was the captain of the losing team. He lost his head. Jun and his mom lost their house, their clothes, and their place in the city.

The small light flickered a bit. We all stared at the straw mats on the floor.

"That's terrible," said Sam.

"I knew that guy was a jerk," said Fred.

I wondered why Jun's mom was telling us all of this. I wondered why Jun had saved us.

"How . . . who . . . what can we do?" I asked.

"You have been sent by the gods," said Jun's mom. She answered like she had heard exactly what I was thinking. "I had Jun rescue you because you can help our city get rid of this man."

"What's the plan?" said Fred. As always, Fred was ready for action.

Jun's mom looked up. I think she had been thinking about this for a long time. The light shone off her simple blue necklace. Sam's mom has one that looks just like it. I realized that's why she looked familiar. She reminded me of Sam's mom.

"Our sacred book tells the story of twin brothers who came back from the dead to challenge the Lords of the Underworld to a ball game."

The darkness of the night outside closed around us. A hooting echoed in the jungle. The hair on the back of my neck rose up.

"Wouldn't it be amazing if you three came back from the dead to challenge the High Priest to a ball game?"

I'm not sure what exactly a jaguar sounds like, but something in the jungle let loose a screaming howl.

The hair all over my head stood up.

● ● ●
(eight)

"I will tell you the story of the ball-playing twins from our sacred book," said Jun's mom. She sat closer on the straw mat and lowered her voice.

"Back near the beginning of the world, the twins' father was a famous ball player. He was so good that it drove the Lords of the Underworld crazy. The Lords tricked the father and killed him."

Jun's mom sipped her chocolate drink.

"The twins grew up. They loved to play ball, too. They also became amazing ball players. When the Lords of the Underworld heard about this, they tried to trick the twins and kill them."

Jun spoke up. You could tell he knew the story, too. "One of the twins got his head cut off. But his brother put it back on, and they came back to win the game."

"Whoa, whoa, whoa," said Sam. "No cutting off heads in our plan, okay? We are magicians, but

I'm not sure we can do the head trick."

Jun's mom laughed. "You won't have to do exactly as the twins did."

"How does any of this help get rid of Kakapupahed?" said Fred.

Jun's mom looked into our eyes. Her black eyes looked like the middle of the night. "This is how it will work. Kaka will believe you have been eaten by the jaguars. Our people believe in the stories of the ball players who come back from the dead. When you three appear tomorrow morning on top of the temple, dressed as ball players, Kaka will have to accept your challenge."

I had a sinking feeling I knew what the challenge would be. But I had to ask. "So what exactly is our challenge?"

"You challenge Kaka himself to a game of ball. He is a terrible player, but he will be too proud to admit it. He will lose. You will be seen as powerful priests and be given *The Book*."

It sounded dangerous, as usual. But I didn't see any other way of getting *The Book* and getting back home.

"Yes!" said Fred. "I like this plan. A little one-on-one. Maybe a game of J-A-G-U-A-R. Kashmuny will crush that Kakapupahed." Fred danced around the room, faking a few dribbles and jump shots.

Jun and his mom looked thrilled.

Sam doodled figures on the dirt floor. He did not look thrilled.

"I hate to be a party pooper, but what is it exactly that happens to the losing team?"

Jun stopped fake shooting with Fred. "Kaka loses his head. Then my mom and I can return to our place in the city."

Sam blinked. I'm sure he was thinking there was a good chance we could be the team losing the heads.

Sam thought for a second or two. Then he said the bravest thing I think I've ever heard Sam say. "Sounds like a good plan. Let's do it."

And that's how Fred, Sam, and I found ourselves hiding in the stone house at the very top of the stone pyramid of Chichén Itzá just before dawn. We were dressed in the loincloths, padded belts, and leg and shoulder pads of the Maya ball players. Sam and I had

41

our hair pulled into a classic topknot with a red-and-white striped headband. Fred had decorated his Knicks hat with parrot feathers.

We found Fred's basketball right where Jun's mom said it would be—on the jeweled jaguar statue at the top of the pyramid. Fred flipped the ball nervously back and forth.

We had gone over and over our plan to surprise Kakapupahed and force him into a game. Now we could only wait for the sun to rise.

"Are we complete morons or what?" said Sam. "What are we doing here? Whose idea was this to help these people out?"

"It was yours," I said. I gave Sam a punch on the shoulder.

Sam pushed his glasses up and smiled. "Yeah, I guess it was. Thought I'd better show this Kaka guy some mad Inurface skills."

The first pink light of the sun lit the morning sky. The birds, beasts, and bugs of the jungle came to life cheeping, squawking, and peeping. A ray of sun lit the top of the pyramid.

"They're coming!" Jun's voice came up the steps from the bottom of the pyramid like he was standing next to us. I still wonder how they did that.

Fred turned his feathered Knicks cap backward. "Game time."

••••
(nine)

Fred, Sam, and I stood at the very top of the pyramid steps—just like we planned. We must have looked pretty sharp in our pads and feathers and black dot jaguar markings.

Kakapupahed didn't see us at first. He was leading a whole crowd to the Jaguar Tree to see what was left of us. Just like Jun's mom said he would.

He reached the giant stone snake head at the bottom of the steps. That was my signal.

"Kakapupahed!" I said in my deepest voice.

Somebody let out a surprised scream. Kaka jumped and looked all around. One of his priests pointed up the steps at us. A few of the people went down on one knee. Two minutes ago, everyone had been going to see our chewed bones. Now, here we were, in full ball-player gear, standing on top of the highest pyramid temple.

The surprise part of the plan was definitely working.

Sam stood with his arms folded. Fred held his ball under one arm. I gave my speech—word for word—just like Jun's mom told me.

"Kakapupahed, we return from the Jaguar Moon with the strength of the Sun."

Right on time, the sun rose higher and lit us and the top of the pyramid.

"We have returned like the ball-playing twins who challenged the Lords of the Underworld," said Sam, saying his line perfectly.

Now the villagers really started buzzing. We could hear them talking back and forth. Fred waited a few seconds, and then delivered the money line.

"Kakapupahed, we challenge you, on this special day of the Harvest Sun Snake, to a ball game."

"What?" said Kakapupahed. He looked left at his priests. He looked down at the people. "How did—"

"Yes, play a game!" shouted someone in the crowd.

"Let the game decide!"

I recognized the voices of Jun and his friends. Other villagers joined in.

"A game, yes."

"Like the twins!"

"Play ball!"

Kaka took a step up the pyramid. He turned back to the crowd. He looked up at us. He looked back at the crowd. He was definitely shook. This was not part of his plan for this big day on the Maya calendar. He stopped still.

I thought, what if he completely freaks out?

What if he just tells his warriors to cut our heads off right now? That wasn't part of our plan.

Fred decided to try one more line of his own. "What's the matter Kaka? Is it true what they say? You've got no game?" Fred spun his basketball on one finger. "I heard you can't even beat the little kids in Maya dodgeball."

Kaka made some weird half-roar, half-yell kind of noise. He looked completely crazy. But he couldn't let us show him up. "We will play ball."

The people gave a cheer. The priests gathered around Kakapupahed and looked up at us. We got our wish.

The full yellow ball of the sun cleared the tops of the trees. It blazed on the top pyramid steps. We got our wish to play against the High Priest. We got our wish to play in his home court.

I looked at the scenes carved in the stone walls. I wondered if it was too late to change our wish.

(ten)

We stood back in the middle of the Maya ring ball court where we had begun our Time Warp adventure. Now that we knew we were playing for our heads, the court looked even bigger than it did the first time. The thought crossed my mind that this might be the place of our final Time Warp adventure.

"Look at those guys," said Sam. Kaka and his two teammates were wearing pretty much the same pads as we were. But they also carried feather-covered shields and carved sticks. They wore bright capes and long twisting headdress pieces.

Kakapupahed stared at us with pure hate. No more fake smiles. His two teammates were even more scary. They looked like they were carved out of pure muscle.

"Don't get psyched out," said Fred. "Stick to our game plan. They are the enemy. We're like the Knicks battling the Lakers."

49

"Those two guys look like they do play for the Lakers," said Sam. "Tell me again why this is such a good plan?"

The people packed into the stands at both ends. It was weirdly just like the pyramid. The Maya builders had made the court so we could hear almost everything being said in the stands. It only made things spookier, standing out alone under our ring.

"They try to put the ball through our ring. We try to put the ball through their ring," I repeated more to myself than anyone. "They play their style with no hands. We play our basketball style with hands."

"And may the best style take over the city and the universe," said Fred.

"And may we please get the High Priest's *Book* and warp ourselves out of here. Amen," said Sam.

"Like cash money in the bank," said Fred.

"Gee," said Sam. "It all sounds so easy. Why do I feel like something is about to go terribly wrong?"

We didn't have time to answer. Drums and pipes played what must have been the Maya national anthem. One of the priests rolled out the ball. The game of our lives was on.

We realized right away that Sam was right. Kaka's

teammates were like NBA pros. We didn't touch the ball for the first five minutes . . . and they weren't even using their hands! They bounced the ball from hip to knee to shoulder, back and forth.

Kaka was as bad as Jun's mom had said. He played like he thought he had skills, but it was his teammates who controlled the play. He was slow and out of shape. We did our best to tangle up the other two players and get in their way so they couldn't get a clear shot at our ring.

A long shot rebound finally bounced my way.

"That's it!" yelled Fred. "Control the ball. We can play three-on-two all day. Kaka stinks."

I jumped to rebound the ball. It flew through my hands, smashed off my chest, and knocked me down. I couldn't believe it. The ball was solid rubber. It felt like a basketball filled with sand.

Sam got a hand on the ball. He took off for their ring. Kaka brought him down with a vicious kick. Sam fell flat. Kaka butt-slammed Sam's head into the ground.

"Ohhhh," groaned Sam.

"How about a whistle, ref?" Fred yelled. Then he remembered there was no ref. Just one of Kaka's priests smiling.

Kaka's teammate scooped up the loose ball on one hip. Neither Fred nor I could get to him. He bounced it, then kneed it all in one move straight at our hoop. Time slowed again—this time in a ter-

rible way. If this shot went in, we were going to lose the game, our heads, and Jun's city—and we hadn't even taken a shot yet.

Kaka stood and laughed, already cheering with both hands over his head.

The ball flew up, and up, and up. It hit straight off the inside edge of the ring, rattled . . . and bounced out! We were still alive.

The crowd cheered, blew pipes, and banged drums. They were on our side.

Kaka stood frozen in surprise. Fred grabbed the rebound and crossover-dribbled right around him. One of Kaka's guys ran to steamroll Fred. He bounce-passed the ball to me. The other guy lined me up for a hit. Sam got to his feet and took off down the right side. I passed the ball to Sam.

Fred was right. We could take these guys three-on-two.

Sam dribbled right under Kaka's team's ring.

The crowd was going nuts. We could hear them chanting.

"Kashmuny!"

"Kikbut!"

"Inurface!"

Kaka's two pros took off after Sam with speed

I've never seen. One guy charged from the right. The other guy charged from the left. They weren't even looking at the ball. They were just going to crush Sam and even the odds to two-on-two.

"Shoot!" yelled Fred.

"Duck!" I yelled.

"Kashmuny! Kikbut! Inurface!" yelled Jun and his boys.

"Fred?" said Sam.

The Maya pros charged.

"Joe?" said Sam.

The Maya pros jumped.

"Aieeeeee!" yelled Sam. He closed his eyes and heaved the ball backward over his head. The two Maya pros hit with a sickening *crunch*.

The ball flew up.

The Maya pros fell back—knocked out from the force of the hit.

The ball flew up, and up, and up . . . and perfectly through Kaka's ring without touching a bit of stone.

The crowd went absolutely nuts.

Fred and I ran over to Sam. He lay flat on his back. His glasses hung from one ear. Blood trickled out his nose. He wasn't moving at all.

"Sam?" said Fred.

"Sam?" I said.

(eleven)

"Sam! Say something," said Fred.

Sam didn't move.

The crowd ran onto the field to celebrate.

"Knuckleheads say what?" said Sam.

"Sam, you're back from the dead," said Fred.

Sam groaned and sat up, fixing his glasses. "Did you get the number of that truck? What happened?"

"Sam Inurface! Sam Inurface! Sam Inurface!" chanted the dancing crowd.

"That was an amazing shot," I said, helping Sam to his feet and dusting him off.

"Shot?" said Sam.

"You won it all," said Fred.

"Oh, of course—my shot," said Sam. "I knew that."

The crowd reached their new hero, Sam Inurface. They lifted him up on their shoulders and

paraded around the court with him. We all marched out into the town.

Kakapupahed, of course, disappeared. The second Sam's shot went in, he ran off into the jungle as fast as he could. He knew what was coming next.

The crowd circled around the square and stopped at the base of the pyramid. They presented us to a group of official-looking guys in the fancy robes and usual feather headpieces. Jun's mother stood next to them, looking as official as all of them. She stepped forward.

"Sam Inurface, Fred Kashmuny, and Joe Kikbut,

you have won the game. You have rid our city of a certain person whose name shall now mean disgrace. For this we give you the honor of the blood sacrifice."

She handed Sam a long razor-sharp blade.

Warriors led Kaka's two losing teammates through the crowd. They still looked dazed from knocking heads. But they were going to meet their end proudly.

"I wha'—? I who—? I—?" Sam looked at the blade. Everyone was watching. He staggered a bit, and leaned over to hold himself up with his hand on the giant stone snake head. Blood dribbled out his nose again. It splashed right on top of the snake head.

The crowd cheered.

Fred and I helped Sam stand up.

"How wise. How noble," said Jun's mom. "The hero Sam Inurface gives his own blood . . . and spares the other team." Jun's mom smiled at Sam with that same familiar look I saw the night before.

"Look! The serpent tastes the blood and grows," said one of the official guys.

We looked at the sun's shadow from the pyramid steps. It looked like a giant string of triangles that connected to the snake's head. And it looked exactly like a snake's body wiggling down the pyramid.

"I what?" said Sam. "I mean—yes, I did. Spare these men. All I ask is that you give us the High Priest's *Book*." Sam lowered his voice so only Fred and I could hear. "So we can get out of here before we have to give any more blood."

Jun's mom pointed to one of the priests. "Go," she said. The guy sprinted up the ninety-one steps and back down in record time. He held out the High Priest's book.

Sam stood up tall and held his nose to stop the bleeding. "Peepuh ub Chichén Itzá, dang you fo dur hep. Dow we mus go homb."

"Home sweet safe home," I said. I took the thin blue *Book* from the priest. I got ready for that funny swirly dropping-down-a-hole feeling of time warping home. It's like waiting for a sneeze. I opened the *Book*, and . . .

Nothing.

No green time warping mist.

"Come on," said Fred. "Quit joking around."

I opened the blue *Book* again. Still nothing.

"Sam," I said. "Maybe you have to write the date again like you did to warp us here."

Sam dropped his blade and picked up a rock to scratch the date:

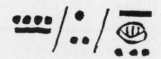

Nothing.

No green time warping mist.

So the High Priest's book wasn't the Maya version of *The Book* after all.

I opened the book for one more try. I looked at Sam and Fred.

We had managed to keep our heads, but it looked like we were going to keep them in the middle of Chichén Itzá, one thousand years ago.

(twelve)

Everybody made a huge fuss over us. Sam was the biggest hero. We were fed tortillas, chili, corn, fruit, roast birds, all the best.

That evening we sat in Jun's old house—the nice one he lived in before You-Know-Who became High Priest.

"Well, if we're going to be stuck here, we'd better start getting things up to speed," said Fred. He picked up a round tortilla. "See, you cut it into sections like this. Bake them. Tortilla chips. Then you dip them in salsa."

Jun and his boys laughed.

"You guys make a great calendar," said Sam. "And the zero is fantastic. But you really might want to look into this thing called 'the wheel.' Very handy invention."

"Let's show them our alphabet," I said. "It's got

61

to be easier than drawing all of those pictures." I drew A, B, C in the dirt.

Jun looked closely. His eyes lit up. "Joe, Sam, Fred. That reminds me. In my practice to become a scribe and priest, I made something for you to remember this day." Jun's mom smiled at Jun, then at us. Jun ran off into another room. He came back with his own book of folded pages, wrapped in a jaguar skin cover.

He opened the book and showed us his work. There were hieroglyphs of Fred, Sam, and me. Sam was shooting the ball. Fred wore his Knicks cap. I was stepping on a High Priest's head.

Jun flipped the page. He had drawn a picture of the shadow snake going down the pyramid.

"Oops, I forgot one thing," said Jun. He pulled out a brush, and put the finishing touch of the date on the bottom of the page.

Jun handed Sam the book. The

faintest wisp of green mist curled out of one corner.

"Is that—?" said Fred.

"It is," said Sam.

"*The Book*," I said.

Jun's new page, with the date, was our Time Warp ticket home.

The green time traveling mist snaked around us.

Jun and his friends looked shocked. Jun's mom calmly raised one hand and waved a small good-bye.

The sun, the moon, the planet Venus swirled around us. We wheeled and wormed through calendar time. We dropped down through the underworld, and flew off into the stars.

(thirteen)

Fred, Sam, and I appeared on the basketball court in Brooklyn exactly when and where we had left. Fred's shot, hanging in midair, bounced off the backboard, hit the rim, and bounced out.

"Darn," said Fred.

Sam wiped a bit of blood off his nose. "Watch and learn from a legend."

"Million-to-one odds says you can't hit that shot again right here, right now," said Fred.

"You would challenge Sam Inurface?"

"Two million to one."

Sam picked up the ball. "Joe, you have got to do something about that *Book*. Why don't you give it back to your uncle? Give it to your sister. Give it to somebody before it kills us." Sam dribbled the ball. "But I was pretty amazing, wasn't I?"

"Oh yeah," I said. "Especially when you dribbled your bloody nose all over the place."

"I was talking about my classic two-hand, no-look, over-the-back swish shot," said Sam.

"I'll bet you anything you want you can't make that shot on this hoop," said Fred.

"Okay, the bet is: for one complete revolution of the Maya calendar, you will be my slave," said Sam.

"You're on," said Fred.

Sam turned with his back to the basket. He closed his eyes.

"So how long is one revolution of the Maya calendar?" asked Fred.

"Fifty-two years," said Sam with a huge smile on his face. He threw the ball two-handed, no-look, over-his-back.

The ball rose up, and up, and up into the air . . . and hung there like the sun, or the moon, over all time.

Professor Sam's Maya Math

The Maya had the whole math and calendar thing figured out way before we were around. Their calendar is still the most accurate calendar ever invented. And they only needed three symbols to write any number.

That's why I'm switching over to all Maya math, and the Maya calendar.

You can, too.

Amaze your friends. Annoy your math teacher. Be more in touch with the cycles of time.

Here's how:

= 0

• = 1

━━ = 5

Forget that old 1, 2, 3, 4, 5, 6, 7, 8, 9, 10. These are the only symbols you need to know.

So the Maya numbers from 1 to 19 are:

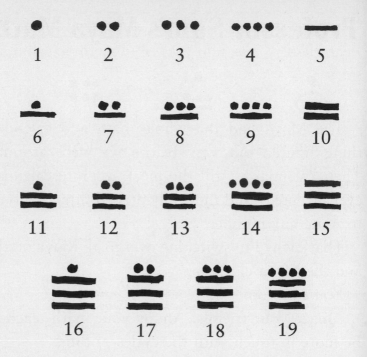

And you know that stuff about place value?

1000s   100s   10s   1s

Forget that, too.

The Maya places go from bottom to top, instead of left to right, and they go by 20s instead of 10s.

8000s   (20 x 400)
400s   (20 x 20)
20s   (20 x 1)
1s

So once you get past 19, you move up to the next place of 20s, and use the same three symbols.

= 20    = 28    = 63

When you get above 399, you move up to the next place of 400s. So

2 (400s) = 800

2 (20s) = 40   } = 847

7 (1s) = 7

Above 7,999 you move up to the next place of 8000s.

It's as easy as counting (on all your fingers and toes) by 20s.

Come back next week for the Maya Calendar.

We'll find out that according to the Maya calendars, the current Long Count cycle that began on August 12, 3114 B.C., will end on December 21, 2012 A.D.

Now that should be some party.

Professor Sam

Turn the page for a special preview of the next

TIME WARP TRIO™

novel:

DA WILD, DA CRAZY, DA VINCI

ONE

"**R**eady! . . . Aim! . . . "

"Wait!" yelled Sam. He fixed his glasses to take a better look. "We're supposed to be in Italy."

Fred, Sam, and I were standing with our backs to a steep, sandy hill. It looked like it could be Italy. But there was a strange-looking invention sitting in front of us—a wooden, flying-saucer-shaped thing, about as big as an ice cream truck.

The size wasn't the scary part. The scary part was the guns sticking out of it. The even scarier part was knowing the word that usually comes after "Ready! Aim!"

"You're lucky we didn't end up in a giant toilet," said Fred. "But now you'd better figure out what to do about those guns pointed our way."

I looked at the wooden flying-saucer tank. Fred was right. Half of its guns were pointed right at us.

1

"Greetings, um, whoever you are in there," I said. "We are peaceful travelers, just looking around for a guy named Leonardo da Vinci. Ever heard of him?"

A man with a short, dark beard, who wore a reddish-colored robe, stepped out from behind a group of small trees.

"Who asks for Leonardo da Vinci?" said the man.

"We ask for Leonardo da Vinci," I said. "I mean me, I'm Joe. This is Fred. That's Sam."

The man stepped closer and looked us over. He was half smiling in a way that looked very familiar.

"This guy had better not be Thomas Crapper," said Fred.

"We're looking for Leonardo da Vinci because

2

we have this *Book*," I said. "And we have a drawing in our *Book* just like one of the drawings from Leonardo's book."

Now the man looked surprised. "You have seen my notebooks?"

Sam figured it out in a second. "Your notebooks? Of course. We *are* in Italy. It is you. You're just younger than you were in that drawing we saw with the white hair and white beard."

Now the man looked very confused.

Sam kept babbling anyway. "I knew it. I knew it. I knew it. Leonardo da Vinci. Leonardo the scientist. Leonardo the inventor. You are Leonardo."

"Yes," said the man slowly. "I am Leonardo da Vinci. You know me. But I don't know you. You seem so young to be spies." Leonardo waved one hand. Two of Leonardo's men came out from behind his wooden tank invention, carrying a long piece of rope. They tied Fred, Sam, and me together.

"It's always the same thing," said Leonardo. "Someone trying to steal my ideas."

"Oh no," said Sam. "We are big fans of yours. We love your ideas. Your giant crossbow. Your cannons. Your submarine. . . ."

3

Now Leonardo looked shocked. "How do you know about these things?"

I saw Sam was getting us deeper in trouble. I spoke up before he could do any more damage. "Oh he's just guessing," I said. "We're not spies. We're inventors too. And we're not from anywhere near here. We're Joe, Sam, and Fred . . . da Brooklyn."

"I don't think I know that town," said Leonardo.

"No, I didn't think you would," I said. "But we came from there looking for a thin blue *Book* with strange writing and drawings and pictures so we can maybe ask you a few questions about how it works and then get right back to Brooklyn and never bother you again, really. Have you seen it around?"

"A notebook?"

said Leonardo. "Blue? With drawings and writing? Like this?"

Leonardo pulled out a thin blue notebook.

We were saved.

Birds tweeted in the trees. Water bubbled happily in the stream. It was a beautiful morning.

"So you do have *The Book*. You are the inventor of *The Book*," said Sam. "This is amazing. It's the first time we ever managed to time warp someplace we wanted to . . . *and* find *The Book* right away."

Even Fred was impressed. "Wow," he said. "And before we warp back home, Mr. Leonardo, I would just like to say you draw some pretty fine stuff."

"Absolutely," I said. "We liked all of your drawings. Even the ones of those strange looking people. Those were weird . . . but good."

"Leonardo da Vinci," said Sam. "Wow."

Leonardo stared at us. Something wasn't quite right.

"So if you could just have your guys come back and untie us," I said, "we'll just ask you a quick couple of questions about *The Book*. How it works and stuff like that. Then you can get back to testing your wooden tank thing."

"No one has seen my notebooks," said Leonardo. He put the small blue book back in his robe. "If you have seen them, you must be spies. And there is only one solution for spies." He stepped back and waved to his wooden tank. It wheeled around sideways so even more guns pointed at us.

"Oh no," said Sam. "This is worse than getting flushed down a giant toilet. Do something, Joe."

Fred struggled against the rope. "Stall them with a trick."

I tried to think of a trick. Any trick.

"Ready! . . . " said Leonardo.

All I could think of was that we had just met the great Leonardo da Vinci.

"Aim! . . ." said Leonardo.

All I could think of was that we were going to get blasted by an invention of the great Leonardo da Vinci.

"FI—"

OWT

Wait a minute. I can't let us end like that. Six pages into the story and the Time Warp Trio gets it? Without any explanation? That's not right.

I have to at least try to explain how three regular guys from Brooklyn found themselves face-to-face with Leonardo da Vinci, somewhere in Italy, somewhere around the year 1500.

It all happened because of inventions.

Well—it really all happened because of one invention.

You probably won't believe it when I tell you this invention isn't a rocket, or any kind of machine at all. It's a book called . . . *The Book*.

I know this doesn't sound like much of an invention. But *The Book* is not like any other book. It's a book that warps time and space. I got it as a birthday present from my uncle Joe. He's a magician. Not a very good one.

The Book is one amazing invention. It has taken Fred, Sam, and me one hundred years into the future and thousands of years into the past. We sailed with Vikings in 1000. We fought Japanese samurai warriors in 1600. We saw the Brooklyn Bridge getting built in 1877. And that was just in the last few months.

The not-so-amazing part of this invention is that we don't really know how *The Book* works. Sometimes a picture sets it off. Sometimes it's words. One time a magic square of numbers got it started. All we know is that when *The Book* starts leaking its pale green time-traveling mist, it takes us to some other time and place.

No time passes at home while we are gone. The only way to get back home is to find *The Book*. And we always seem to get in trouble no matter where we go.

So like I was saying, this time warp is all about inventions. That's what got us into trouble. It all started Saturday morning with a mysterious message from Sam:

MEET ME IN MY WORKSHOP FOR THE ANSWER TO EVERYTHING. BRING *THE BOOK*.

8

Fred and I met Sam in his room in the apartment where he lives with his mom. He calls it his workshop. He also calls it his lab, his library, or his control room. It all depends on what he's working on. Fred and I don't ask him why. We just know he's weird.

This time Sam's room—I mean workshop—was covered with posters, drawings, and diagrams. Those giant illustrated books of warplanes and tanks and battleships were stacked everywhere.

"This time I've got it," said Sam. "This time I've really got it."

"Got what?" said Fred. "Bad breath? You've always got that." Fred whacked Sam on the head with his NASCAR hat. Sam was so intense, he didn't even notice. He pointed to a drawing in one of his books.

"Here is the answer to all of our Time Warp problems."

"Really?" I said. "This is the answer to how *The Book* works? Why we can never hang on to it? When it's going to send us time warping?"

"Yes, yes, and yes," said Sam. "All those things."

I looked at the drawing.

"Sam," I said. "This is a drawing of a toilet."

"Good answer," said Fred.

"Not that drawing," said Sam. "I mean the whole book. The whole idea. Look." Sam flipped through *The Book*. "It's a book about inventions. The telephone, the car, flying machines, bubble gum, Velcro, even toilets."

Fred started drawing his own invention—a hot rod. "I call my latest invention The BeastMobile."

"And who would know the most about how these inventions work?" said Sam, still ignoring Fred.

"Uh . . . rocket scientists?" I guessed. "Guys who write encyclopedias?"

"No," said Sam. "The guy who invented the thing."

Fred drew a giant rat driving his invented dragster. "And so a toilet is the answer to all of our time warp problems? I don't get it."

"Forget the toilet," said Sam. "Do I have to explain everything? We find the person who invented *The Book*. That way we find out the answer to how it works."

I took *The Book* out of my backpack. It's a small book really. Blue cover with weird silver designs. Kind of light. You wouldn't think it's as powerful as it is. I put it carefully on the edge of Sam's desk.

"I never thought of that before," I said. "It just might work."

"Of course it will work," said Sam. "Alexander Graham Bell could tell us how the phone works. Thomas Edison could tell us how the lightbulb works. Thomas Crapper could tell us how the toilet works. . . ."

Fred looked up from his drawing. "Are you kidding me?"

"No," said Sam. "The inventor of *The Book*

11

should be able to tell us anything we want to know about *The Book*."

"I mean, are you kidding about a guy named Crapper?" said Fred. "That can't be for real."

Sam opened one of his books and read, "Thomas Crapper, a London plumber, born in 1836. Though Alexander Cummings is generally credited with inventing the first flush toilet in 1775, Mr. Crapper and his plumbing business most likely gave us his name as a synonym for 'toilet' or 'bathroom.'"

"Too bad for him," said Fred.

I moved *The Book* as far away from Sam's book as possible. "Let's not get *The Book* too close to anything we might be really be sorry for," I said.

Fred pinned his finished drawing on Sam's wall. "I think for once in his life, Sam has got a good idea. But how do we find the inventor of *The Book*?"

"Right here," said Sam. He pointed to a picture of an old guy with long white hair and a long white beard. "Leonardo da Vinci."

Fred and I looked closer at Sam's book. There was the drawing of Leonardo, surrounded by his paintings and other sketches from his notebooks.

"Isn't he the guy who did that Mona Lisa painting?" said Fred.

"Exactly," said Sam. "And he drew all of this other stuff."

Fred held his drawing next to a Leonardo sketch of an ugly bald guy with a huge nose. "Not bad."

"But I don't get it," I said. "Leonardo was an artist. How does that make him the inventor of *The Book*?"

Sam picked up another one of his giant books. "Leonardo was a famous artist. But he was also an amazing scientist and an *inventor*. Did you know he made drawings for a helicopter? And a submarine? And a tank? All way back around 1500. And look at this."

Sam dug through more of his library books. He had that wild look in his eye he gets when he's on to something.

"I've done the research. The man was a genius," said Sam. "He must have been the one who invented *The Book*."

"Sure Sam," said Fred. Fred pointed to his head and twirled his finger around in the universal sign for crazy.

"There," said Sam. He flipped open a book to one of Leonardo's drawings.

"Sam," said Fred. "I'm no genius, and I can draw better than that. It's a naked guy with four arms and four legs."

"No, you moron," said Sam. "It's Leonardo's drawing that solves the problem of turning a square into a circle. And look at Leonardo's backwards writing. I think he used this to hide the secret of time warping."

"I think it shows you've finally cracked," said Fred. "Tell him, Joe."

I couldn't tell him anything because I was standing there with my mouth open.

"Joe?" said Fred.

I stared at the Leonardo drawing. I couldn't move.

Fred helped me the way he always helps. He whacked me on the head with his hat. "Snap out of it."

"That drawing," I said. "I think it's the same one that's on the inside cover of *The Book*. And it has the same backwards writing."

I opened the front cover of *The Book*. There was Leonardo's drawing and the writing.

"I knew it!" said Sam. "Look, right here it says 'ᴛһɑпk Υou, Тimе Ԝɑгр Тгio'."

14

"Whoa," said Fred. "So Leonardo da Vinci invented *The Book*?"

I saw the first wisp of pale green mist drift out of Leonardo's drawing.

"I guess we'll find out soon enough," I said.

The mist grew thicker and began to circle around Sam's workshop.

Fred suddenly looked panicked. "The mist came out of the da Vinci drawing, right? Cause if it came out of the Thomas Crapper drawing, I will make an invention to give you both a smackdown."

The green time-traveling mist thickened and swirled around and around like . . . well, like . . . a toilet flushing.

I thought I heard a faint roar and a whoosh.

And we swirled down the drain of time.